Run Far, Run Fast

for Mandy, sapere aude

LIBRARY OF CONGRESS CATALOGING-IN-PUBLICATION DATA

Decker, Timothy.
Run far, run fast / Timothy Decker.—1st ed.
p. cm.
Summary: When the plague comes to her medieval town,
a young girl must flee to find sanctuary.
ISBN-13: 978-1-59078-469-3 (hardcover : alk. paper)
[1. Black Death—Fiction. 2. Plague—Fiction.
3. Middle Ages—Fiction.] I. Title.
PZ7.D35754Ru 2007
[E]—dc22   2006039102

Front Street
An Imprint of Boyds Mills Press, Inc.
815 Church Street
Honesdale, Pennsylvania 18431

Run Far, Run Fast

TIMOTHY DECKER

Front Street

Asheville, North Carolina

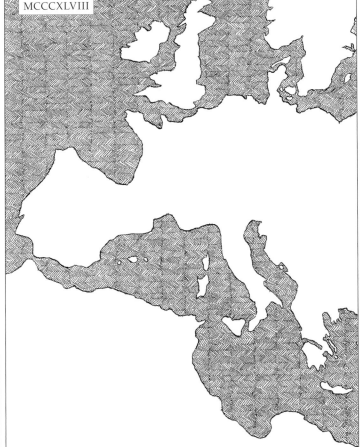

MCCCXLVIII

I will tell you the story of one small girl in a time of great fear. Kings and countries were being laid low by an illness that struck all manner of living creatures.

The girl lived with her father, who was a carpenter, her mother, and her little brother.

The town where the girl lived was not far from the mountains or the sea. It was surrounded by farms and had a busy market.

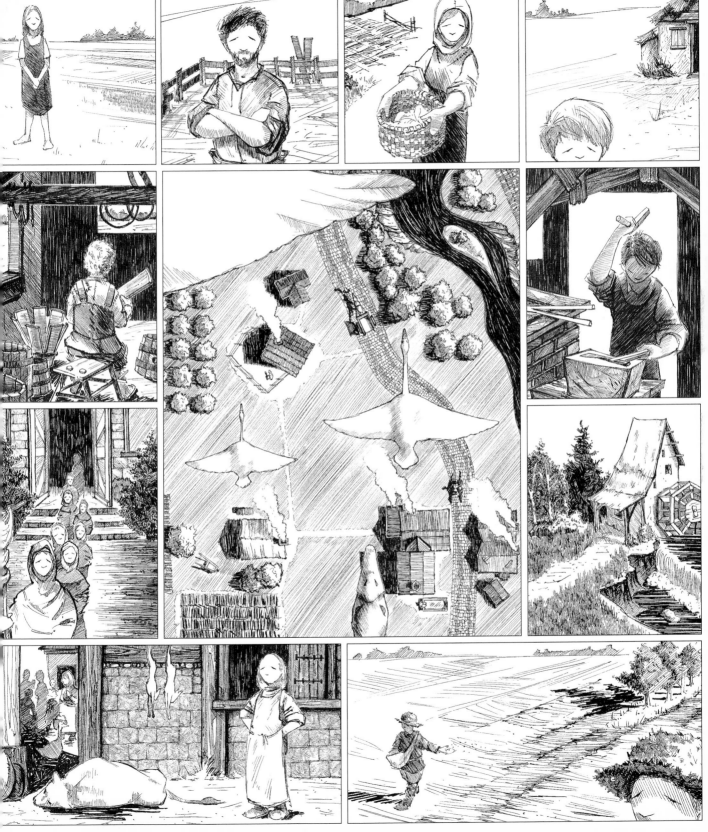

Every year was the same until her tenth summer.
The Pestilence entered the girl's world like a tide.

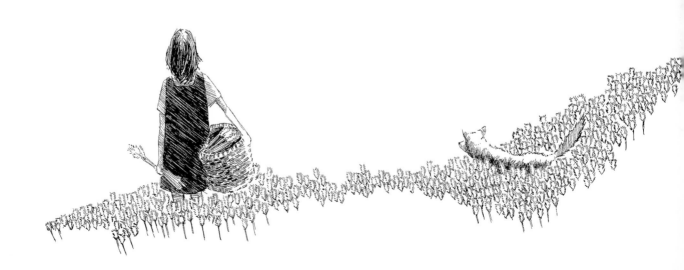

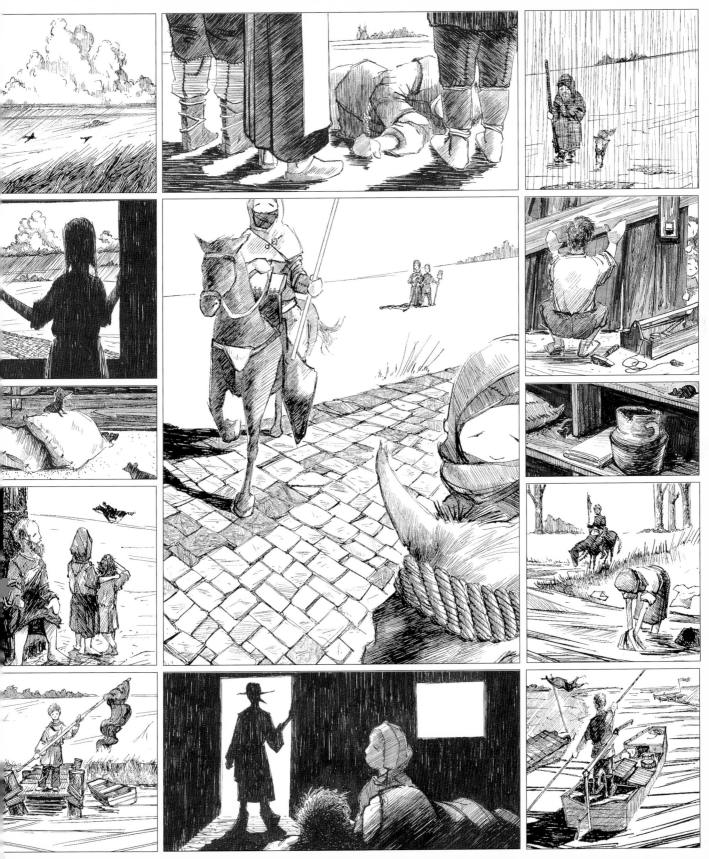

One afternoon, three men came looking for her father. Her mother said he was in the forest and would be gone for days. They did not believe her. So she told them he was sick and resting. The men left.

Soon boards were nailed across their doors and windows. They were told that food and water would be brought to them. With sunset came silence. After dark the mother knocked the boards off a window, kissed the girl's forehead, handed her a small bag of food, and lowered her into the night. She whispered, "Run far, run fast."

The girl was afraid to walk alone at night or to sleep
in the forest, so she followed the road along the river.
An old monastery loomed above the trees.

Eventually, the road led to a city by the sea. A soldier told her the gates of the city were locked to keep the Pestilence out. But the Pestilence was already in the city.

The girl continued down the road. She met many travelers. There were pilgrims, tradesmen, and even great armies. Most paid no attention to her. Some helped her. The road passed untended fields and through empty villages.

The girl learned as she traveled.
She saw people do strange things,
things she did not understand.

The road led to another city, one
with low walls made of stout timber. A
soldier told her the city gates were
locked to seal the Pestilence within
the walls and thus protect others.
But the Pestilence could not be caged.

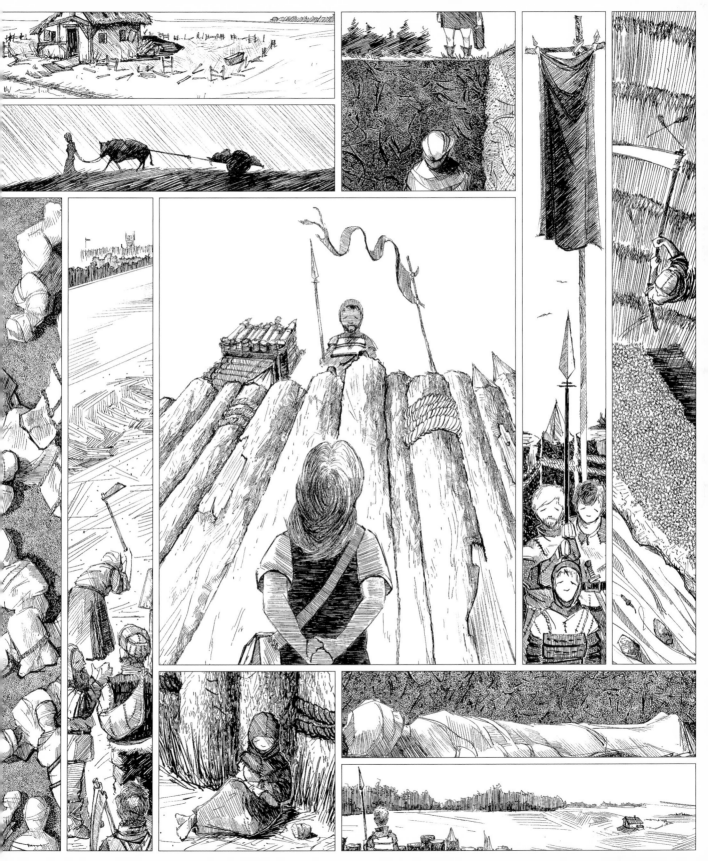

The girl walked back into the forest where she was no longer afraid. That is where we met. I took off my hat to show her that I was a man. We shared my food and talked. She asked many questions.

I told her that some people thought the Pestilence came from the planets twirling in the heavens. Others believed they were being punished for their sins. I told her that I did not know what the Pestilence was, but I reasoned that it was part of Nature, as death was a natural part of life.

Many cures were believed to ward off the Pestilence: eating strange things like gold and precious stones, sniffing flowers and other good smells, and traveling to holy places. But neither riches nor knowledge nor faith seemed to matter.

The Pestilence swept away all that was. When it passed,
when the fear and confusion ebbed, only sorrow remained.
Still, the girl wanted to help her family. I gave her
food and told her where she could find me.

Her home was empty. She asked a man if he knew where her family had gone. He didn't but he said that as more and more people fell ill, they were taken to a building on the edge of town—the pest house.

From a thicket, she saw a man guarding the door to the
pest house. She scrambled through a window. The room was dim
and alive with the breathing and coughing of the sick. She tiptoed
among them, whispering the name of her father, her mother, and
her brother. Her brother called to her. She grabbed his hand
and ran with him out the door and into the woods.

I was surprised to see them walking up the path to my home. I fed and cleaned the children, then put them to bed.

This is how the girl and boy entered into my household. We will discover what the world wishes to show us in the morning.